Also by Seth Edgarde

Hart Island
The Devil Speaks Hungarian
Blood Sunrise
St. Louis Blues
Brick City Blues
Lumina

LADY
OF THE
LAKE

SETH
EDGARDE

BLACKBIRD BOOKS
NEW YORK · LOS ANGELES

A Blackbird Original, December 2017

Manufactured in the United States of America.

The events and characters depicted
in this book are fictional.

Cataloging-in-Publication Data

Edgarde, Seth.
Lady of the lake / Seth Edgarde.
p. cm.
1. Roommates—Fiction. 2. College graduates—
Fiction. 3. Santa Monica (Calif.)—Fiction. I. Title.
PS3605.D4564 L33 2017 813'.6—dc23 2017962842

Blackbird Books
www.bbirdbooks.com
email us at editor@bbirdbooks.com

ISBN 978-1-61053-042-2

First Edition

10 9 8 7 6 5 4 3 2 1

LADY
OF THE
LAKE

She was a big girl, at least 5'11, with shocking curves and a smile you couldn't take your eyes off of. People always noticed her, especially men, even in Los Angeles, with all the willowy blondes and wannabe actresses.

There was something about her, wholesome and happy, Midwestern, but still fun and playful. Part of it was the way she moved, confident and deliberate, but not self-conscious, like an athlete who knew her trade and did it by second nature.

She *was* an athlete. She had played basketball for Minnesota Tech on an athletic scholarship. It was a weak team, but it was still Division I, and she was the starting point guard. They'd gone to the tourney when she was a junior and advanced to the second round on her 37-foot jump shot at the buzzer against New Mexico State, her moment of glory. But they got demolished by North Carolina by thirty points in the second round, never making it to the sweet sixteen or even the tourney again.

She was still crowned "Lady of the Lake"—homecoming queen at Minnesota Tech—her senior year. It was a funny title to outsiders, but in Minnesota and on that campus, it made perfect sense. The land of 10,000 lakes—actually 13,000 any native will tell you with pride—one of which was right there on campus.

Shrouded in school tradition and known simply as "The Lake," it lent its name to the school's sports teams: The men were the Minnesota Tech Lakers, and the women, the Lady Lakers, no post-modern sensibilities able to penetrate the depths of that glacial water or those traditions.

For her part, she loved it. She loved being the homecoming queen, loved playing basketball, and loved the traditions. Her boyfriend used to call her the happy camper. Even after an indiscretion on the road with a booster for the men's team, where he was the star, she forgave him. She had three brothers. She understood those urges. It was still just about the only time anyone saw her cry, except when her grandmother died.

Rick. The homecoming king. Everyone had figured they'd stay together. But he wanted to go pro, and she wanted to go to California. Campus legend held that if a girl walked around the lake twice with a boy, they would be together forever. They did one walk as king and queen but never got around to that second time.

Now he was playing in Europe, and she was in Santa Monica.

Everyone called her Liz back then. The coach said it sounded better and looked better in print in the game programs and newspaper clippings. She was ok with it but was happy to be back to Betsy now. *Betsy Jenkins.* It did sound a little funny for a basketball player. *Liz Jenkins.* Yeah, the coach was right.

She was far away from all that now, living by the beach in Santa Monica, dressing up every day, working for a luggage company as a junior associate—whatever that meant—and living in a three bed, two bath apartment with four other people, all, like her, fresh out of school and trying to make their way.

She made a point of telling people that she wasn't in sales, even though, strictly speaking, that wasn't true. She was in management, really just a grunt trainee on the lowest rung of the ladder, but she was too beautiful to stash away back in a cubicle there on the ninth floor, with that big smile, smooth, even skin, dark brown hair, and clear green eyes. So they started sending her out to greet clients with the sales people. She liked it, liked being with people, and they liked her, big, happy, and easy on the eyes. And never threatening.

So she worked with the sales team, peeling off from her spreadsheets, reports, and training manuals for long enough to help with the latest sale. "It's good for me, mom," she'd tell her mother back in Minnesota, always on her cell phone, out in the hall, on her way back from lunch.

"I miss you, sweetie," her mother would tell her.

"Me too, mom." Then she'd pause. "I love you." Then she'd add quickly, "Tell daddy I love him too." And she'd smile, a little teary-eyed, before heading back in for work.

It wasn't what she wanted to do for the rest of her life—working for a luggage company—but it was good for now: Putting her degree to good use, learning about business in the real world, making money, living the California life. And she liked the people there, warm and friendly, plus it was only two blocks from the beach and two more in the other direction from her apartment. And the hours were more than reasonable: She was never there after five and she would sometimes even take long lunch breaks to go and exercise, stopping home to shower on the way back. No one seemed to mind. Especially on Wednesdays, which were always slow.

One particular Wednesday, she was just about to head out when she remembered that there was a farewell lunch for one of the techies who she knew from the training program. She was debating whether to go or not, when another woman from her group caught her eye, with three more in tow.

"Tim's last day," she said. "Are you coming?"

She hesitated. Then one of the guys smiled at her. "Come on!" he said in a teasing way. Then they all joined in, and she broke into a grin. No escape.

She had wanted to go for a run, maybe even stop by the gym and do some weights, and now she was at lunch, on her second beer, slightly buzzed, joking with the guys at her end of the table.

They ordered dessert, a blueberry cobbler à la mode, and she made eye contact with the waiter, tall and thin—an actor, probably—who looked a bit overwhelmed. She gave him a smile, and he gave her one back, a little moment to tell him not to worry, they'd be out of his hair soon. She wanted coffee but decided not to heap one more brick on his load.

He was back with the cobbler a minute later, and unsure who to give it to—they had ordered it to split, there at her end of the table—he began to lay it down in the middle.

The two guys on either side of her reached for it at once, and, for a moment, all three—her two co-workers and the waiter—had their hands on it at once. Then a moment of embarrassment, then they each released their grip, with one pull a little too forceful, and then a failed and comical attempt to catch the bowl in mid-air which served only to move it directly over Betsy's lap and flip it over.

They all watched as it disappeared over the edge of the table, face down, into her lap.

LADY OF THE LAKE

She jumped back, startled, feeling the weight of it on her thighs, remembering how it felt to skinny dip into the lake back at school at the first spring thaw—another campus tradition—as she felt the cold ice cream then the hot, syrupy compote seep through the fabric of her dress, through her pantyhose, to her skin, burning and freezing at the same time, then seeping into her crotch and through her underwear.

She slid back instinctively and stood, holding the bowl in place and then moving it slowly upright and sliding it up along her dress to catch most of the gooey mixture, white and blue, with purple stripes, back in the bowl. Looking out over the table, holding the bowl, she saw everyone staring at her, agape, the waiter now looking up at her, over six feet, even in flats, his mouth open.

She put the bowl on the table as white dripped off her hem and onto her black shoes.

Suddenly the waiter sprang to life, pulled off his apron, and went to wipe her dress.

"That's okay," she said, gently grabbing his wrist and stopping him from carelessly touching her most sensitive areas in a vain attempt to undo the damage.

Then she took a napkin and began wiping off what she could, feeling thick, syrupy drops hit her ankles and noticing the white speckles on her shoes.

Wiping under her hem, she turned the napkin and wiped her shoes, which seemed no worse for the wear.

Then she looked up to see four or five people offering their napkins, wet and dry, just a bit too serious, and she smiled at the group. "Dessert's on me," she said, with that big toothy grin, and everyone laughed, except the waiter.

She looked at him. She was a good three inches taller than he was and probably weighed a bit more too. He was whiter than that vanilla ice cream. She had noticed his name tag before. Dave.

"Don't worry, Dave," she told him, still smiling, "I was looking for an excuse to go home early."

He finally exhaled and pushed out a smile. "Well, don't *you* worry, I'm going to get you another one and take it off the bill." His smile faded a bit, but he had regained his composure. "And the next time you're in, lunch is on me."

LADY OF THE LAKE

She and a couple of the other people at the table chuckled when he said *on me*, but he and the others didn't seem to get the joke. Then he disappeared to get that other cobbler, and, still standing, she looked down at the damage.

She had done a pretty good job cleaning it up. It was a white print dress with a fruit pattern, and the white and blueberry stains almost looked like they belonged at first glance. But she felt it moving slowly down the inside of her left thigh and seeping further into the crevice at the top of her leg. It was almost room temperature now but drying fast, sticky, gross, and uncomfortable.

"Hey, it looks like part of the design," one of the jokers at the other end of the table said, echoing her own thought.

"Maybe I should charge the dress maker for enhancing their product," she added.

Then she realized, she needed to get home as soon as possible if she had any hope of saving that dress.

One of the other women, a middle-aged secretary whose name she couldn't remember but who reminded her of her mother, seemed to pick up on it. "Honey, you better treat that right away." But her expression seemed to say it was hopeless.

Nonetheless, she took that as the final bit of permission to leave the lunch and go home to change. She was glad to make her exit before the waiter got back and she'd have to face another awkward moment.

A minute later, she was out on the street, walking the two blocks to her apartment. She felt a little embarrassed, food covering her dress like that, and when a guy looked her over, she made quick eye contact and forced out a little smile, unsure whether he was gaping at the dessert she was wearing or checking her out or both.

She thought about it for a second and laughed. *I can't believe that happened! My roommates are going to tease me about this forever.* She let herself into the apartment. She wasn't used to it being empty. *A nice change of pace.*

It was one of those apartments that always had a steady stream of people coming and going. Maybe it was just happenstance or maybe it was the two pretty girls who lived there or the handsome brothers or just the festive atmosphere, but it seemed to be the focus of a lot of people's social lives.

They had cable with all the channels and a big screen TV, for one. And there was a mellow, happy vibe about the place: California cool crossed with Midwest wholesomeness that made people want to hang out there.

She liked it, and she liked her roommates, but she was glad it was the middle of the day and no one was there. She made her way back to her bedroom—she was the only one who had her own room.

Somehow, she managed to have the best-paying job of them all, enough to cover a full third of the rent and get the back bedroom all to herself, including the adjoining bathroom.

The two brothers, Rich and Bill from Encino, fresh out of Cal State Northridge, were sharing the far bedroom. Jane and her boyfriend Nick, who'd been dating forever and were also from the Midwest—Ohio—though there was no use trying to explain to the natives that the Midwest was big, and that Ohio and Minnesota were not the same place—were in the bedroom between.

The four of them generally shared the bathroom in the hall, but she let Jane use the one in her bedroom when she wanted more privacy.

She filled the bathroom sink with warm water, threw in some liquid Tide, then unzipped herself and slipped out of her dress. Stopping to examine it for a second, she shook her head, grimaced a little, then shrugged before putting it in and gently working the fabric. It wasn't very expensive, but she liked it, and, looking at the pattern, she wondered if, after it was washed, the stains *wouldn't* actually look like they belonged.

She threw out her hose, added her panties—white, of course!—to the sink, tossed her bra in the hamper, and, seeing the sticky blue mess all over her crotch and the tops of her thighs, decided on a shower.

When she was done, she felt much better, and thinking about the whole thing again, she started to laugh. *That poor waiter! I hope his manager didn't see.*

She dried herself off and hung her towel. Suddenly thirsty, she started for the kitchen, still naked. But then she thought better of it. The place was empty. It always was in the middle of the day. But people did come in and out—she did have four roommates—and she knew there were a couple of other people with keys. She had actually given one to her boyfriend, Donny, so she couldn't complain.

So she grabbed her towel and wrapped it back around herself before leaving her room. She didn't like wearing a towel wrapped around herself—it barely covered her boobs and her butt—but better safe than sorry.

Walking out into the hall, she felt it start to slip. Looking down to secure it, she kept walking, focused on the task—a towel too small for a tall girl. Then, a noise. Right there in the apartment. She wasn't alone! She jerked her head up. A person on the couch. She wasn't the type to shriek, but she felt a bolt of adrenalin shoot through her from head to toe.

The towel dropped, and she turned to face the threat, only to recognize him a second later, as she stood there, full-frontal, between the couch and TV. Rich's friend, Brian. She didn't even know his last name. And now she was standing there completely naked, right in front of him.

He stared at her as expressionless and shocked as she was.

He looked her over and smiled with a kind of innocent admiration, and, as if by reflex, she smiled back. She knew he was having a rough time. He'd lost his job, then his girlfriend dumped him. And then his dad died unexpectedly. She'd seen him there in the apartment, wind knocked out of his sails but trying not to show it, and she had tried to cheer him up. She could tell from the way his eyes moved and the way he smiled whenever he saw her, that he liked her. Of course, he knew she had a boyfriend, so there was no point in pursuing it.

But now she was there, right in front of him, buck naked, a little balm on the wounds of his life, and he seemed to appreciate it.

Only a second had elapsed when his eyes met hers again, and they were both still smiling like it was nothing.

"Are you going to pick that up?" he asked, eyes darting down to the towel on the floor then back up to her face, taking in all the rest on the way, almost daring her to leave it.

"Maybe I won't," she said, her mischievous streak aroused, those two beers still working their way through her system.

She wasn't sure why she'd said it—just some playful banter, maybe, keeping it light—but now she had to follow through. Towel still crumpled on the carpet, she turned and walked around the corner, into the kitchen, and out of view.

She got a glass out of the cupboard, filled it with tap water, and drank it half down. Then she walked back out, glass in hand, and nothing else.

She could tell he was trying not to react, to keep it going, to keep seeing her in all her god-given glory. And it made her want to oblige.

So she drank her water and walked slowly back into her bedroom, turning once, at the last minute, to see if he was still looking. When their eyes met again, she let out a giggle, somewhere between surprise, delight, and embarrassment.

She thought about it as she squeezed into her jeans, safely behind her door. *God, Brian saw me naked! And I didn't do anything to stop him! What would my mother think? What would Donny think?* But it was all innocent, she thought. We're all just people. And it seemed to lift his spirits. So no need to feel bad about it.

As she tucked in her shirt and straightened her pockets, she thought about it some more. Rich must've given him the keys. He probably wanted to watch the Warriors' game on ESPN. He was from up north and a fan of all the Bay Area teams. And that made her think about basketball and how much she missed playing.

When she went back into the living room, he was still there. He looked disappointed, and she tried not to look him in the eye, but she couldn't help herself. And when she did, they both broke out in grins all over again, and she felt herself blush a little.

"We have to stop meeting like this," she said, playful and a little flirty, but still keeping it light.

"Any Wednesday?" he asked, his tone as playful as hers.

She had to think for a second before she put it together. It was a movie. She'd watched it on TCM last week. There were a bunch of people there, as usual, but she couldn't remember if Brian was one of them. He must've been. All she could remember was that Jane Fonda was in it,

LADY OF THE LAKE

and she was holed up in an apartment in New York, and it was a comedy.

"Only if I can be Jane Fonda."

He looked surprised, surprised that she remembered, put it together so quickly, and kept the banter going. "Well, you've got the body for it."

Now she really did blush. Still smiling, appreciative at the flattery but embarrassed, she turned to go, when he called after her.

"See you next Wednesday."

Huh? she thought, before she realized that he was just being cheeky. Or maybe even hopeful. She turned her head and grinned at him, "Maybe you will." Then she turned back and left. She didn't know why she'd said it. She wasn't sorry for her little show—it was harmless enough, and she knew it made him feel better—but she had no intention of repeating it, either next Wednesday or ever.

You're a bad girl, Betsy Jenkins! She thought to herself, laughing at the thought of the whole thing—blueberry cobbler in her lap, that dropped towel, and a free show for Brian. She certainly wasn't going to tell Donny. He'd go crazy.

By the time she got back to work, she'd almost forgotten about it. She had three messages on her phone and a dozen unanswered emails, mostly from potential customers, but a few filtered through from the complaints department. She got stuck with that too, fielding complaints. It was that sweet, calm, Midwestern voice. But it never bothered her. She always liked talking with people, especially if she could help them with a problem.

So she picked up the phone and returned her first call. And she listened to a two-minute tirade.

"How about we just replace the bag for you?" she told the woman on the other end of the line.

"I guess that would be okay," she said, her anger as least partly diffused.

It was ridiculous. Yes, she knew what a lifetime warranty meant, but the airline had lost her bag. It was amazing how many people called about stuff like that. She'd gotten in trouble the first time she'd done it—replaced a lost or stolen bag—but then the higher-ups realized that it didn't actually cost the company much, and it was good business: *We know it's not our fault, but it's not yours either, and we know how frustrating and traumatic it can be to lose your luggage. So have a new bag on us!*

It didn't get her a promotion, but it did get her more face-time with customers. They liked her: big and friendly, smart and pretty, and she even liked to talk sports. She had just the right combination of traits to make men want her but not want to try to take advantage of her and women like her but not feel threatened by her.

She wound through her emails and phone calls, until it was almost five, and she was ready to leave. Then the calendar in her phone dinged, and she remembered: She had drinks scheduled with a client for after work.

It was with a middle-aged couple who ran a travel shop in Downtown L.A. She probably could have gotten out of it, since they were local and could reschedule, but she wasn't going to try. *Don't let the customer down if you don't have to,* her professor used to say. So she went, even though she wasn't quite dressed for it, having changed from her work clothes into jeans after the cobbler incident, as she came to call it.

"Don't worry, it's L.A.," her co-worker, Debbie, told her.

"Easy for you to say, you're from here," she said. Then she let out a smile. "I'm from the Midwest. You know how uptight we are." Then she winked at her, and Debbie smiled back, even though she didn't quite get the joke.

So she met her clients for drinks in her jeans and blouse, and they talked travel gear and luggage, then family and friends. She liked them— Bob and Cynthia Metcalfe, running the same shop on Olive Street for almost twenty years. It turned out he was from Pittsburgh, and she was from right there in Santa Monica. They had lost a daughter who would be about her age, and it made her want to cry.

"We have a new line, lightweight and very funky, in all different colors. I'll get you a great price," she told them, changing the subject before she actually did cry.

They liked her too and ended up treating her to dinner. She didn't get home until almost ten and was surprised to see Brian sitting in almost exactly the same spot, only now the couch was full with Rich, Bill, and a woman she didn't know.

She made eye contact with Brian, who looked up at her, innocent but warm. "Hey, you're just in time. There's a good movie coming on. It's by the same guy who did the Jane Fonda movie last week."

The woman chimed in, "Robert Ellis Miller. They're doing a retrospective. Tonight is *Sweet November*." There was an odd pause, and the woman stuck out her hand. "Grace. I'm a film student at USC."

"No, sorry, I can't. Not tonight." She looked at the five of them on the couch, hanging out like they were back in college. She had been naked in front of Brian a few hours before, and now it was all so normal, like it never happened.

"Oh come on! Watch with us! We ordered a couple of pizzas," Bill said, trying to talk her into it.

He was a fun guy but a bit of a mischief maker, and she wondered if he didn't know something.

"No, no. I haven't seen Donny all day," she said, glancing briefly at each of them, including Brian, who showed no reaction.

So Bill shrugged, and she walked off, avoiding any more eye contact with Brian, afraid she'd give herself away.

She was expecting Donny to be there in her room. He had texted her earlier, saying he'd meet her there, back at the apartment, but the room was dark and empty. She called and got his voicemail then texted. A minute later came the reply. It turned out he had to work even later than she did. He was an associate at a trading company downtown and got stuck with odd assignments on a regular basis. They all did, he reassured her, but she was always a little suspicious. Still, she was annoyed that he hadn't told her earlier, that she had to text him to find out.

But she decided not to let it bother her. So she went back out into the living room and plopped herself down on the chair adjacent to the couch just in time for the movie. She liked it even more than the one with Jane Fonda. The woman in this one, Sandy Dennis, acted as a sort of therapist, a curative, for men with troubles. She kept looking over at Brian—no girlfriend, fired from a dead-end job at a sandwich shop on the Promenade, just lost his father—and wondering about that afternoon. *Silly, just silly,* she thought. But still, it got to her.

Donny finally came over very late. She was already in bed. She had really wanted to talk, but it was past midnight, and she was drifting off to sleep. Still, she turned and smiled, glad to see him. She hadn't seen him since Sunday afternoon and missed him. She usually only saw him a couple of times during the week. He had his own place, shared with only one roommate, but it was small and dirty, just over the border in L.A., a first floor apartment on an alley with bars on the windows, in a borderline neighborhood.

So he stayed over at her place when he could. That meant Friday and Saturday nights for sure, and sometimes Sunday night. But they both worked during the week, so it was harder.

She was surprised when he wanted to have sex. But also relieved. She wasn't really in the mood, as he started to pull her pajamas off, but she could see how ready he was. *No, definitely not cheating,* she thought.

When they were done, he lay on top of her, not quite asleep, still inside her. So she stroked his hair and held him a little longer until he moved off and went to sleep. It took her longer to get to sleep. She hadn't quite managed an orgasm, but it was good. Very good. And now she was awake. But before long, dreams took over and thoughts of Sandy Dennis and Anthony Newley in that apartment in New York. And the four of them on the couch, watching, mesmerized. Rich and Bill and Grace and Brian. Brian who'd seen her naked. And then, before she realized what was happening, it was morning again.

She had forgotten about her dress, which she'd left hanging in the shower. It was almost dry, but she could see the stain against the print pattern. She wondered if she'd be able to wear it again as she threw it in the laundry basket before showering, brushing her teeth, and getting dressed for the day. She wore a blue pantsuit, as if she were preparing for another blueberry cobbler incident.

Donny was still asleep when she got out of the bathroom, and she had to wake him up. He was in a bad mood—he wanted to sleep—but he would be late if he didn't get a move on. And then, she realized, he wanted something else too, when he grabbed her ass.

No way, she thought, his hands grabbing her butt from the bed and pulling her hips down towards him there on the bed. But she pushed him off, with a little more authority than she'd meant to.

"I'm sorry; I've got to go. I'm going to be late," she told him, putting on some chap stick and then turning back to him and squeezing out a smile. "And so are you."

He fell back in bed, resigned to his fate.

"See if you can get out earlier tonight, and I'll make you dinner, and we can have some fun," she said, smiling even more, even though sex was the last thing she wanted just then.

But it seemed to keep him at bay, and a moment later, she was out of the apartment and heading to work. It was a short, pleasant walk, only a few blocks down Santa Monica Boulevard, away from the ocean, to a short office building.

She had a full plate for the day: a training manual to edit, a lunch meeting, and a slate of phone calls. Each day seemed to melt into the next, and she wondered where it was all going. But she liked her co-workers, the money was great, and she still couldn't believe that she could walk to work in 65 degree weather in November.

She had just managed to take her seat in her third floor cubicle, when Debbie leaned over.

"Dean got fired this morning," she told her, grinning.

"What?!" she looked up concerned. "What are you talking about? They love Dean!"

"Yeah, well, you know how we're not supposed to trade the company's stock until after the quarterly report comes out?"

"Yeah . . ."

"Well he did, and he got caught, and they fired his ass!"

Neither one of them liked Dean. He hit on all of the women in the office and talked shit about them behind their backs.

Unsure about whether to really believe it or not, Betsy kept her enthusiasm in check. "But the earnings were terrible last quarter. Why would he buy stock?"

"He didn't. He bought options betting the price would go down, and it did. Apparently he made a shitload of money, but he's going to have to give it all back."

"Oh my god! How did they find out?"

"They can track it through your social security number."

Betsy stood up without even logging on and went to get breakfast over in the kitchen. She caught sight of a folder on Debbie's desk. There was a piece of paper sticking out of the top. She couldn't believe it. A memo from the office manager and VP in charge of marketing reminding everyone about the rules for trading company stock.

When she told Donny later, he shook his head. "He should have had his girlfriend do it in her name."

Her mouth was agape, and he let out a big grin, letting her know that he was only kidding. *Maybe.* He was from New York—practically a foreign country to her—and she was never quite sure that they were on the same page. Still, she loved him and figured they'd eventually get married, though there was a nagging doubt that never left her.

She'd forgotten about it all by the time Sunday rolled around. It was her favorite day. Softball in the park with Donny, Deb, and a bunch of other friends. They had their own team and had a joined a league. Then it would be off to brunch, back to the apartment for a shower, then maybe a movie, dinner, and an early evening to rest up for the week.

On this particular Sunday, though, she was in a bit of a funk, sitting there on the bench with Deb, waiting for the game to start, wondering what she was doing with her life. "I sell fucking luggage," she complained to her friend. It wasn't like her: To be blue, to use that kind of language, even to have that kind of self-doubt.

"Hey, I've been there longer than you!" Deb said, and they both laughed. "But I'll tell you a little secret." Then she looked her in the eye. She had big, bright blue eyes and wore bright red lipstick over full lips, even out on the softball field. "I'm not sticking around too much longer."

"What?!"

"Don't tell anyone," she said, suddenly lowering her voice and looking around. "I'm applying to grad school at UCLA."

"No way!" Then she paused, curious and happy but a little envious, but still earnest. "In what?"

"Social work. I'm applying for an M.S.W. Maybe I'll even go for a Ph.D."

"That's awesome," she said. *I need to do something like that,* she thought. *Get my life on track, help people.* She looked down then back up, and she seemed to sense that Deb knew exactly what she was thinking at that instant.

She was still thinking about it Monday morning but was too busy with sales calls by the afternoon. And then another dinner meeting with drinks, and before she knew it, the week was half over.

Usually, she was able to squeeze in a midday workout at least twice a week, but she wasn't sure she'd even get in one this week. To make matters worse, she hadn't had time after work, because of the meetings. Then, sitting there in her cubicle, all of a sudden, her boss had gone to lunch, her phone stopped blinking, and her sales calls were done.

She shot out the door and changed at the gym. It was only a block away, and she did sometimes see coworkers there, but nobody cared. That mellow California lifestyle. She rode the exercise bike, watched bowl game predications on ESPN, and did some weights.

As she walked back to her apartment, she vaguely realized it was Wednesday. And when she walked in, there was Brian, sitting there on the couch, watching the very same show on ESPN, sitting there like a puppy dog waiting for his biscuit. She wasn't expecting it, but she should have been. *What is he thinking? I have a boyfriend. It was a one-time deal; I'm not that kind of girl!*

But before she could say anything, he looked at her, as surprised as she was. "Sorry to keep crashing your place. I didn't think anyone was going to be here. I'm having kind of a bad day." Then he started to get up. "I'll go."

She didn't know whether to believe him or not. He sounded like he was telling the truth and didn't seem to expect anything. If anything, he sounded embarrassed. And really did look down in the mouth.

"No, sit!" she said. "I just came to shower up. I won't bother you."

"You sure?"

"Yeah, absolutely."

As she walked down the hall, she wondered if he was watching her. She turned around and glanced halfway back at the last possible moment before closing her door, enough to see him looking only at the TV, never realizing that he had been watching her the whole way up to that point.

And she suddenly felt terrible for him. She wished she could find him a job. And a girlfriend. As she stepped out of the shower, she remembered the week before and grinned. She dried herself and wrapped herself in a towel—awkward as always, barely covering her big girl body.

She was thirsty after her workout and wanted to go out to the kitchen for a glass of water but realized that she couldn't go out in a towel. So she took the towel off and hung it up. Then, on an impulse, grinning even wider, she walked out into the hall and back down to the kitchen, right past him, in front of the TV, there, again, stark naked.

She gave him a sideways glance as she went about her business, coming back out into the living room a minute later with nothing but that glass of water. Then she looked right at him and smiled. "Oh, I didn't realize you were still here!"

His mouth hung open, as the man on ESPN blathered away about the Rams chances against the Steelers in the upcoming game on Sunday.

"Well, I'm just going to pretend I'm alone," she said, turning and walking back down to her room without ever looking back.

When the door was closed, she laughed as she got dressed. *Oh my God, I can't believe I just did that!* She thought. *Again!* But she was even less sorry than last week. She knew it made him happy, cheered him up, a private little mid-week boost to a guy who was down on his luck. And who was it hurting?

When she came out of her room, fully-dressed, on her way back to work, she acted like nothing had happened.

She was almost out the door when he spoke up. "You going to watch the movie tonight?" he asked.

"What movie?"

"*The Heart is a Lonely Hunter.* It's the next movie in the Robert Ellis Miller retrospective."

She looked uncertain.

"Rich and Bill and that girl Grace from USC are going to be here." He said it like *he* were inviting *her* to *his* apartment.

"Oh yeah, right," she said, thinking that *he* sounded like the film student. "Sure, I'll be here," she added. "See you later."

Then she was out the door and gone.

By the time Ben Mankiewicz was introducing the movie on TCM, she was back in her usual seat, and Rich, Bill, Grace, and Brian were squeezed onto the couch, ready for the latest.

It wasn't what she expected, even more so than previous film, and it affected her. She felt profoundly sad at the movie's end and didn't want to be alone. Donny still wasn't home, so they all sat around and talked like they were still in college, having a late night gab session.

"It was just so awful," she said. "You know, that he was deaf . . . and when he tried to talk . . ."

"Don't you think that it's just a trite deconstruction of our tradition-centric modes of communication in a post-modern society?" asked Grace.

SETH EDGARDE

Betsy stared at her blankly for a second, before Bill took her attention. "Well, I just have to say that as a gay man, I found the homoerotic elements of his relationship with Antonapoulos to be absolutely fascinating."

"You guys are so full of shit," Rich chimed in.

Bill waved him off. "Oh fuck off! You just want to screw Sondra Locke."

And on they continued. Then one by one, they went to bed. And it was just Betsy and Brian.

"That movie, it just made me feel awful," she said.

"I know," he added. "You just want to do something to help someone like that."

She looked him right in the eye. "Yes."

"Yeah, but what? How?"

She shrugged, a little sad. "I don't know."

And just like that, they were talking about what they could do to help people and make the world a better place. "I mean that girl Grace, why is she in film school? What's that going to do for anyone?" Betsy asked.

"Nothing," Brian shrugged. "If I went back to school, I know what I would go for," he said.

She perked up and leaned in, chin on hand, elbow on knee, her interest piqued. "Tell me."

"Psychology. I always wanted to know about what makes people happy or sad, what makes them do the things they do."

"Well, why don't you go back to school and become a psychologist? I bet you'd be great at it."

He smiled. "Thanks. I have my degree from San Jose State, but it's just a bachelor's. You need at least a master's to do anything real."

"Tell me about it. I wanted to be a nurse like my mother, but I ended up getting a business degree and working for a suitcase company."

Then Donny walked in. It could have been awkward, but it wasn't. She jumped up, smiled, and gave him a big kiss. "You missed a great movie, but it was a little sad. We were just talking about it. Rich, and Bill, and Grace were here until a minute ago." A little white lie.

"Had to work late again. It's a real drag, but if this project flies, I'll be the golden boy."

She put her arm around him, and they headed back to her bedroom. She turned and gave Brian a mischievous smile. "See you next Wednesday." And he grinned from ear-to-ear.

A few minutes later, and Donny was in bed fast asleep with Betsy lying there next to him. She nudged him and whispered in his ear. "I'm so horny." And his eyes popped open.

It was some of the best sex they'd ever had, and it helped to dispel some of the lingering doubts she had about him. When she woke next morning, she had the urge to call in sick, but she didn't.

Then it was the weekend again, and then Monday. And then, before she knew it, it was Wednesday.

It seemed like there wasn't going to be a good time to slip out, but finally, her boss left for a late lunch, and she wound up her last call. When she left, the phone was ringing, but she let it go to voicemail.

There was no time for a workout, so she headed straight back to the apartment. It was after two o'clock, and she wondered if he'd still be there. He was.

"It's so hot out," she said. Then, one piece at a time, her blue pantsuit came off. She didn't do any kind of striptease. She just undressed like she was alone. And she could see that it drove him crazy with delight. Then it was just a white thong, until she took that off too, flinging it on the couch. She wanted to tell him that she rarely wore a thong—they weren't that comfortable—but she was planning to work out in spandex and didn't want panty lines. But she kept her thoughts to herself.

She suddenly realized that she hadn't had lunch and was hungry.

"Want a peanut butter sandwich?" she asked, walking into the kitchen. "I'm starving."

"No thanks. I'm good," he said.

A minute later, she emerged, pb & j in one hand and a glass of milk in the other. She ate standing. Then, finally, she sat on the couch, crossing her legs, canted on one cheek, careful not to touch the couch with her privates, finishing her sandwich and milk, watching the ESPN football highlights.

She didn't look over at him, sitting there on the opposite end of the couch, but she felt oddly close to him. She could hear him breathing and knew he was looking over at her out the corner of his eye. When she was finished, she picked up her clothes and got dressed right there in front of him.

"What's the movie tonight?" she asked.

"The Baltimore Bullet with James Coburn and Omar Sharif."

She smiled at him as she threw her bag over her shoulder. "See you then."

There was an awkward moment, like they were going to hug, but they didn't, and she turned and left.

On her way back to the office, she smiled to herself. She didn't feel a bit bad about it. She needed to shake things up. And she was.

When she got back to her cubicle, Deb leaned over. "Boss wants to see you."

A cold rush went down her back. "Miriam?"

Deb nodded, working those oh-so-expressive eyebrows into a piece of art, as if to say, *Sorry kiddo, been nice knowing you. Say 'Hi' to Dean on the way down.*

She walked around the maze of cubicles until she reached the offices along the side hall, thinking about how twenty minutes before, she was parading around naked in front of Brian when she was supposed to be at work, and now she was getting called on the carpet. And she prayed she wasn't going to get fired. *I'm lucky to have such a good job, and here I've been complaining about it like an ungrateful child. If I just make it through this, I'll never complain about this job again!*

When she got to the door at the corner office, she took a deep breath and knocked. No answer. So she knocked again.

"Come in!"

So she opened the door and stepped in. She'd only been in there once before, with several other trainees for a meet-and-greet on her first day. She was alone this time and took it in in full. It was a big office with lots of glass and light on the outside walls and bookshelves half-filled on the other two. She could see a crystal tablet marking the company's IPO and listing on the NASDAQ in 1995. And behind that was Miriam Dobkin, mid-fifties, somewhere between plain and pretty, jet black hair—dyed, no doubt—short and straight, contrasting against a pair of small but vibrant blue eyes.

There were pictures of her husband, son, and daughter on her desk in front of her and diplomas on the wall off to the side. An MBA from Harvard and bachelor's in something from Bryn Mawr.

The woman behind the desk smiled at her, gesturing to the chair. "Please, have a seat."

She came around and sat on the edge of the desk. She had wide hips and a more feminine build than she was expecting. And she sensed a certain warmth, also unexpected.

"I just want to let you know how pleased we all are with your work." She leaned in to her. "In fact, you're our number one associate." She leaned back and stood. "It's always a gamble with new associates. It becomes something of a culling process. We have to let people go. But you've got a bright future here if you want it." She paused for a moment then sat back down on the corner of the desk. "You've got a bright future wherever you choose." She looked at her with motherly warmth. "I love your spread-sheets. You're extraordinarily meticulous in your accounting work, and the clients adore you." Then she smiled right at her. "And I hear you're quite a softball player."

"Thank you," she said, somewhere short of stunned.

A minute later, she was out in the stairwell on the phone with her own mother. She had meant to call her before heading back into the office, but she was running late. She could hear the pride in her voice when she told her of the glowing review, and the pain in her voice when she told her how much she missed her. She had had the urge to tell her about Brian, but she would never do that. It would be impossible to explain, and she didn't want to try. Somehow it all coalesced to make her feel warm and loved.

She had dinner with Deb after work. They talked about the company and how it would be to stay and try to rise up through the ranks. Deb seemed genuinely happy for her. Betsy asked her about the application to UCLA and how it was going. "Everything's in, and I've got my fingers crossed," she said, holding them up to show her.

Betsy had almost forgotten about the movie but still managed to make it back in time for the start. When she walked in, Brian lit up, and Bill seemed to notice, even though they were both trying to hide it.

"Welcome!" said Rich. "Have a beer," he added, gesturing to a pair of sweating six packs sitting on the table.

So she grabbed a can of Budweiser, popped the top like an old pro, and kicked back, feeling especially good as she drank her beer and watched.

The other four seemed disappointed in the film, but Betsy liked it. It was light and happier than the last couple of movies, and she was always a sucker for anything to do with sports—even a movie about pool hustlers.

"You know, I'm a pretty good pool player," she said, downing the last of her second beer and feeling the buzz.

"Yeah, I bet you went around beating all the boys," said Bill, snarky as always.

"Maybe I did," she said, a little drunk and smirking.

"Well, I thought the film was boring," said Grace in an uncharacteristically terse comment.

Brian shrugged, not wanting to contradict Betsy's opinion. And Rich, already past his third beer, was asleep on the couch.

With that, the party broke up, and Betsy waited in her room for Donny. It was almost one by the time he texted to tell her he wasn't coming. She thought she would burst she wanted to tell him about her day so badly.

She ended up not seeing him until the softball game on Sunday. She knew he was working on a big deal with the New York office, but they had hardly even spoken all week. He promised that he'd make it up to her after the game, that they'd have a nice brunch and spend the evening together. He told her *he* had some exciting news to tell *her*.

But they ended up spending the afternoon in the emergency room. One of the guys from the other team slid hard into second base and tore his knee open on a stray shard of glass. The bleeding was terrible, and Betsy sprang into action with a tourniquet and a makeshift dressing, cleaning the wound out with a tampon at a nearby water fountain. "They're sterile," she explained. "You ought to be a nurse," Deb told her, not realizing how hard the remark hit.

When they were finally back home at her place later that night, Donny sprang it on her: "They want me to move to New York."

"That's terrific!" she said without hesitating, and she meant it. Then it occurred to her that it meant he'd be on the other side of the country. She'd think about that later. For now, she pushed it down and gave him a big hug and a kiss. "I love you," she said.

And he looked straight at her with those sparkling eyes—blue like her boss but so much nicer—and said it. "Come with me." And she waited for the rest: "We'll get a place, live to-gether."

Her face fell. "Live together!"

"Yeah. It'll be great."

She didn't really want to get married just then, but she didn't want to live together either. She was confused and hurt and needed time to think. She hadn't intended to tell him her news just then—she didn't want to take away from his news—but she blurted it out.

He didn't seem to get it. "But you're not even being offered a promotion," he said.

"Well, no, not right now."

And suddenly, she was being cross-examined. The conversation went downhill from there.

"Look, we're both tired. We'll talk in the morning," he told her.

And she nodded.

But they woke up late, and there was no time to talk, just the morning rush. By the time the week was half over, they had barely even texted once or twice.

When she checked her afternoon appointments before heading out to lunch one day, she realized it was Wednesday again. Brian. She wasn't in the mood for it. His long face and those yearning eyes. But then she thought about Donny, and it made her mad.

Still, she wasn't going to go, until she got a text from Bill, of all people—a group text—telling everyone that it was the second to last movie tonight, a film called *Reuben, Reuben,* and he hoped everyone could make it.

And she realized that she couldn't show up for the movie if she didn't show up and at least talk to Brian beforehand. And she *wanted* to watch the movie. She liked Brian. If she was having problems with Donny and what to do with her life and career, why should she take it out on him? After all, their little get-togethers were harmless enough, and they seemed to be helping him.

So she went back and took off her dress for him. And the rest. It was strange, because it was so un-sexual for her, and she had a hard time telling what he was thinking exactly. But their odd ritual made her feel closer than ever to him, even though she wasn't exactly attracted to him.

Even so, she was beginning to feel oddly comfortable around him with or without clothes, even talking to him through the cracked door while she used the bathroom.

"I've got to go back to work," she said, smiling at him and touching his arm. "I'll see you to-night."

It meant nothing to her, but she could feel his arm tense up.

She brought the beer, and they ordered pizza—one pie, plain, and one with pepperoni. The movie was better than last week, but it un-nerved her. She didn't like poets, and Tim Conti's Scottish accent was strange. And she wasn't sure how she felt about his illicit affairs and insulting wit.

They talked about it afterwards. She tuned out Grace and was amused at Bill's contrarian banter, always clever, never deep. Rich was asleep again. It was Brian who cut to the bone. "I felt bad for him, but you have to take responsibility for yourself. In some way, he deserved what he got."

Yeah, you're right, she thought, though she never said it.

They were still talking when Donny came in. She wasn't expecting him and was still mad but smiled and kissed him anyway.

Later, back in her bedroom, he sat down next to her on the edge of the bed. He took her hands and looked into her eyes. He started off beautifully. "Look, I love you. And I want you with me."

She felt her heart melt. If only he had stopped there.

"But either way, I'm going. It's too big an opportunity. And if you can't recognize that—"

She'd had enough. "Oh, I get it. If I'm too stupid to hitch my wagon to you—on your terms—than to hell with me!"

SETH EDGARDE

He didn't contradict her. "You've got nothing going here. I mean you're selling suitcases."

The tears were coming down her cheeks, but they were angry tears. She knew her cheeks were red, and the words were coming out a million miles an hour. She was standing now, but he was still sitting. He got quiet and looked stunned. Then so did she.

Finally he stood and took her hands. "I really do love you, and I want you with me."

She wanted to tell him how confused she was, but all she could manage was a look down and a nod.

There was hesitation, like *what happens next?* It was somewhere on the cusp of the best makeup sex ever or him going home, and that being the end of it. And she decided.

When she woke up that morning with his leg between hers, with his scent all over her, tasting him in her mouth, she looked into his face, still asleep, and was at peace with herself.

She told Miriam that morning. She was disappointed but told her that she understood and that she'd always have a place there if she wanted to come back. Deb told her that it was the right decision, even though she wasn't sure if she believed her.

Bill gave her a big hug and asked when she was leaving. "Next Friday morning," she told him, realizing that she was actually going to miss him.

"Oh good," he said. "You'll make it to the last film."

And she did. It was a movie called *Hawks* with Timothy Dalton and Anthony Edwards.

She took the day off that Wednesday to run errands and pack for the movers, who were coming the next morning. She wasn't sure about Brian, but when she got home, there he was. She needed to change anyway, so gave him one last show, packing her two suitcases and moving boxes as she undressed, used the bathroom, and made herself lunch.

Then in a moment of indiscretion even by their standards, she stood there, naked in front of him, and he kissed her. She suddenly *felt* naked, and went back to her room and changed, ready to go back out for a few last errands.

The kiss had jarred her. She didn't regret it, but she was glad she was with Donny and glad she was leaving. It had broken the spell, because they had broken the rules. A fun game. You can look, but don't touch. But he touched her too, resting his hands on her hips. It wasn't much, but she knew that she wouldn't be able to continue even if she stayed in L.A.

When she came back out, he was gone.

Later, when they were all sitting around watching the movie, he didn't seem to want to make eye contact with her. Then, when it was over, she finally caught his eye, and he smiled at her, and she knew that somehow she'd helped set him back on track.

She didn't see him after that, and before she knew it, she was in a U-Haul with Donny, and they were driving out of town. She thought to look back at the old apartment but never did.

NEW YORK CITY, FOUR YEARS LATER

She stepped out of David Geffen Hall and looked for her husband. She loved going to the symphony—it was something totally new for her, one of the many things that he had introduced her to—but hated the long lines at the ladies room during intermission.

There he was, holding a drink, facing the courtyard, looking out over the Koch Theater and the New York City Ballet, with the Metropolitan Opera to the right.

There was a man approaching with a woman on his arm. The way he moved and cocked his head drew her eye, and she realized.

"Brian!"

And he looked right at her. "Oh my god, Betsy!"

Just then, she put her hand on her husband's shoulder as he turned to the sound of her voice and looked at her.

"This is my husband, Sean," she said, and she could see the look of satisfaction in his eye. Then, looking at Sean, "This is my friend Brian from L.A."

The men shook hands, and then Brian looked back at her and they locked eyes for a second still smiling—grinning almost—and he gave her a *What happened to Donny?* look. She knew what he was thinking.

"It didn't work out with Donny," she said. "He was kind of a jerk."

"Thank god," he said. "You were way too good for him."

She laughed. Then she looked over at the woman he was with, suddenly realizing that she was already looking right at *her*.

"Oh my God, Grace!" Her mouth hung open. "Are you two—"

"One year this November," she said, holding up her left hand and showing her ring. "I was teaching film up at Columbia, and Brian was a grad student in psychology, and we ran into each other on campus, and here we are." Then she paused. "I'm still teaching, and Brian has a practice in Brooklyn."

She sounded different. More mature, less pretentious, and Betsy found herself liking her for the first time. Then she told them: "I went back and got my nursing degree, and I'm working as a rehab nurse at the Rusk Institute here in midtown." She sounded like such a New Yorker, she could hardly believe it. Then she looked over at Sean. "We met at a fundraiser." She didn't tell them that he was on the board.

He was a bit older than she was, almost twenty years, but they had clicked instantly and got married less than a year later. She didn't care about the fact that he was rich, but she didn't mind either.

As the four of them stood there, the chime rang signaling the end of intermission. She thought to exchange information but then thought better of it. There are some relationships that are complete the way they are.

"Well it's great seeing you both!" she said.

They smiled and nodded. They all seemed to sense the same thing.

As the couples parted, with Grace and Sean looking the other way, she caught Brian's eye one last time and gave him the thumbs up. He mouthed the words *you too,* and she held her husband's arm and turned and walked away with him.

"They seem like nice folks," he said.

She looked up at him—he was even taller than she was in heels. "I used to walk around naked in front of him," she said, smiling, just short of mischievous.

He looked surprised. "You slept with him?"

He seemed to know that Brian wasn't her type.

SETH EDGARDE

"No!" she said. "He was in a really bad funk, so I'd get undressed for him and walk around naked to cheer him up." It was the first time she'd said it like that. "I guess that sounds ridiculous."

"Not at all. That would certainly cheer me up!"

And she laughed and held his hand tightly as they headed back in for the second act.

To see our other great titles,
visit us at:

BLACKBIRD BOOKS
www.bbirdbooks.com